ZONE

This book is due for return on or before the last date shown below.

1 8 JUN 2013		
25 OCT 2013		
17/10		
4/1		
1 7 FEB 2017		
0 4 NOV 2019		

GU00854719

Out of the Fog
by David Orme
Illustrated by Jorge Mongiovi and Ulises Carpintero
Cover photograph: © appletat

Published by Ransom Publishing Ltd.
Radley House, 8 St. Cross Road, Winchester, Hampshire, SO23 9HX, UK
www.ransom.co.uk

ISBN   978 184167 461 2

First published in 2011

Copyright © 2011 Ransom Publishing Ltd.

Illustrations copyright © 2011 Jorge Mongiovi and Ulises Carpintero

Originally published in 1998 by Stanley Thornes Publishers Ltd.

A CIP catalogue record of this book is available from the British Library.

The rights of David Orme to be identified as the author and of Jorge Mongiovi
and Ulises Carpintero to be identified as the illustrators of this Work have been
asserted by them in accordance with sections 77 and 78 of the Copyright, Design
and Patents Act 1988.

CONTENTS

Fog at the cottage   5

The empty car   11

The wreck   15

Just in time   21

Back at the car   27

NOT FOR THE PUBLIC TO KNOW

TOP SECRET

ZONE 13 FILES ONLY

FOG AT THE COTTAGE

The fog lay thick on the fields and marshes. It was like a white wall. Elly and Ben looked out of the cottage window. They couldn't even see the trees at the bottom of the garden.

'Why did Dad want to come and live in a place like this?' groaned Ben.

'You've said that a hundred times already,' said Elly.

'I know, but why did he?'

Elly and Ben were staying with their father.
Their parents had split up. They usually lived
with their mother in her flat in London. They
had come to spend a week with Dad in his
cottage in Essex. They both thought it was the
most boring place in the world. It was miles

from the nearest town. Even the village was a
long walk away.

Dad came in from the kitchen.

'What do you want to do today?'

Dad was an artist. He painted pictures of
sea birds. The cottage was perfect for him.

Outside were mud flats stretching out to the sea. They were covered in birds, but today you couldn't see them. You couldn't see anything.

'I want to go down to the village shop,' said Elly. 'But we can't go in this.'

'Why not?' said Dad. 'As long as you stick to the road, you can't get lost.'

Ben and Elly put on their coats. Anything was better than sitting indoors.

THE EMPTY CAR

It was hard work walking back from the village. Dad had remembered that they were out of food and had given them a long shopping list. They had to carry four big bags of shopping home.

'Dad's really mean,' said Elly. 'He could have brought us in the car.'

The fog wasn't quite so thick now. There was a breeze, and the sun was trying to shine.

They saw something ahead of them on the road.

'It's a car!'

'It's Dad's car. He's coming to meet us.'

The car was by the side of the road. Its lights were on. The driver's door was open. The car radio was playing.

There was no sign of Dad.

They walked round to the driver's side. There was a terrible smell.

'What on Earth is that stink?'

They both stared in alarm. There was smelly slime all over the road by the car door. It made a trail leading towards the sea.

It looked as if a giant slug had gone that way.

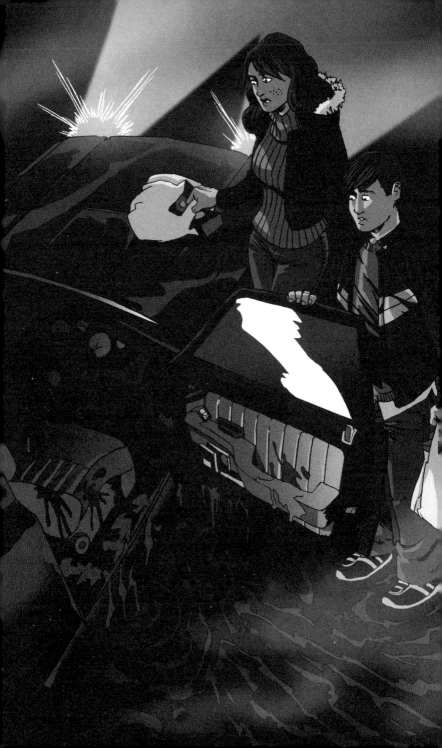

NOT FOR THE PUBLIC TO KNOW

TOP SECRET

ZONE 13 FILES ONLY

THE WRECK

'Something horrible has got Dad!' shouted
Ben. 'Come on!'

They dumped the shopping in the car and
started to follow the stinking trail.

The fog was still lifting. The wind was
pushing it out to sea. They ran over the shingle
beach. The trail was easy to follow.

'Look!'

Ben was pointing ahead. In the distance, they could see two figures. One of them was carrying a body over its shoulder.

'Dad!' Elly whispered.

It was getting difficult to follow the two figures now. The sand and shingle were turning to mud. Elly and Ben were wearing trainers, and they sank down at every footstep.

'Look at their footprints!' whispered Ben. 'They've got feet like ducks!'

The creatures that had taken Dad didn't look like ducks. They were tall, and upright like people. But their footprints were like duck's feet – only much bigger.

'Webbed feet!' said Elly. 'That's how they can walk across the mud!'

'I know where we are now. It's the wreck!'

They had seen the wreck before. They could see it from the windows of the cottage. It was an old fishing ship. Years ago, it had been left to rust away on the mud flats. The creatures were heading for the wreck.

What were they going to do to Dad when they got there?

NOT FOR THE PUBLIC TO KNOW
TOP SECRET
ZONE 13 FILES ONLY

JUST IN TIME

The creatures disappeared into the wreck. A minute later they came out again – without Dad. They turned and headed across the mud towards the sea.

'Come on, Ben. We've got to try and get inside that wreck!'

It was very difficult. The mud was even deeper now. It seemed to be trying to suck off their shoes. Elly nearly lost hers twice. To make things worse, the tide was coming in.

The channels were filling up with water. They remembered that the wreck was covered with water at high tide.

At last, they got to the wreck. One end of it was rusted right away. The other end still had a roof and sides. They saw a rusty door.

The door was hard to pull open. The handle was slippery with slime. They managed to get the door open by pulling together. A terrible smell, even worse than the slime, poured out.

Light came in through a hole in the deck above. Three shapes were lying on the floor. One of them was moving. It was Dad!

Ben and Elly looked at the other two shapes, then wished they hadn't. They were both human, but they had been in the sea a long time. They were white and swollen. Parts of their faces had been eaten away.

Ben and Elly both held their breath and tried not to look at the bodies. They lifted Dad

out into the open. He was tied up with bands
of tough, jelly-like stuff. One band covered
his mouth.

Ben found a piece of rusty iron. He managed
to cut through the jelly with it. Dad seemed O.K.

'Thank goodness you two came along! The tide was coming in fast. Another few minutes and I would have drowned in there!'

They started back across the mud. It was getting even more difficult to walk.

'What are those creatures? What were those bodies doing in the wreck?'

'I've no idea,' said Dad. 'Whatever kind of creatures they are, I nearly ended up as their dinner!

'I thought of you struggling home with the shopping. I decided I would come and meet you. When I saw two figures in the fog, I stopped because I thought it was you.

'I suppose that wreck is where the creatures keep their food. They capture people, then leave them to drown and rot. Then they come back and eat them!'

Ben, Elly and Dad struggled on through the mud.

Behind them, they heard a sound.

The two creatures were following them.

5

BACK AT THE CAR

They had nearly reached the shingle beach. If the creatures had caught them in the mud, they wouldn't have been able to escape.

'Quick!' yelled Dad. 'Back to the car!'

They rushed up the beach. The creatures were getting closer. Ben, Elly and Dad got to the car and jumped in. They slammed and locked the doors. Dad tried to start the engine – but nothing happened!

'The battery's flat!' groaned Dad. 'I left the lights on!'

The two creatures were by the car now. They were human in shape. Their skin was grey and slimy, like a slug. They had huge, fish-like eyes and two holes instead of a nose.

One of them picked up a heavy stone from the beach. It started to smash the car windows with it.

Elly remembered something they had bought in the village. It was a bottle of bleach, with a spray top. She grabbed it and squirted the bleach through the broken window, right into the eyes of the creatures.

They both screamed. Elly watched in horror as their eyes seemed to melt away. They staggered over the road.

A truck was coming the other way. With a thud, it ran over both of them. They lay still, just a slimy mess on the road.

Later that night, the fog was thick once more. Six creatures came up out of the sea, and stood looking at what was left of their friends.

With anger in their huge eyes, they headed for the cottage.

About the Author

David Orme is an expert on strange, unexplained events. For his protection (and yours) we cannot show a photograph of him.

David created the Zone 13 files to record the cases he studied. Some of these files really do involve aliens, but many do not. Aliens are not everywhere. Just in most places.

These stories are all taken from the Zone 13 files. They will not be here for long. Read them while you can.

But don't close your eyes when you go to sleep at night. **They** will be watching you.